J
598
Roc   Rockwell, Anne F.

EASY   Our yard is full
                of birds

Our Yard Is Full of Birds

by Anne Rockwell

illustrated by Lizzy Rockwell

Macmillan Publishing Company   New York

Maxwell Macmillan Canada   Toronto

Maxwell Macmillan International
New York   Oxford   Singapore   Sydney

For Nicholas

Text copyright © 1992 by Anne Rockwell

Illustrations copyright © 1992 by Lizzy Rockwell

Macmillan Publishing Company, 866 Third Avenue, New York, NY 10022

Maxwell Macmillan Canada, Inc., 1200 Eglinton Avenue East

Suite 200, Don Mills, Ontario M3C 3N1

Macmillan Publishing Company is part of the

Maxwell Communication Group of Companies

Printed and bound in Hong Kong   First Edition

10   9   8   7   6   5   4   3   2   1

The text of this book is set in 18 point ITC Modern 216 Light.

The illustrations are rendered in watercolor and pencil.

Library of Congress Cataloguing-in-Publication Data

Rockwell, Anne F. Our yard is full of birds / by Anne Rockwell;

illustrated by Lizzy Rockwell.—1st ed.   p.   cm.

Summary: Describes the variety of birds visiting a yard,

from the phoebe and wren to the crows and blue jays.

I S B N 0-02-777273-X

1. Birds—Juvenile literature. [1. Birds.]

I. Rockwell, Lizzy, ill.   II. Title.

QL676.2.R63 1992 598—dc20   90-30436 CIP AC

Our yard is full of birds.
There are birds in the trees
and on the lawn
and in our flower garden.

The phoebe sits on the stone wall
by the garden
and wags its tail at me.

A wren lives in the little birdhouse
my father helped me build.

A pair of cardinals lives
in our tall pine tree
all year long.
They are always together.

Shiny speckled starlings like to perch
in the treetops.

They squeak and whistle and squawk.
Then they fly away.

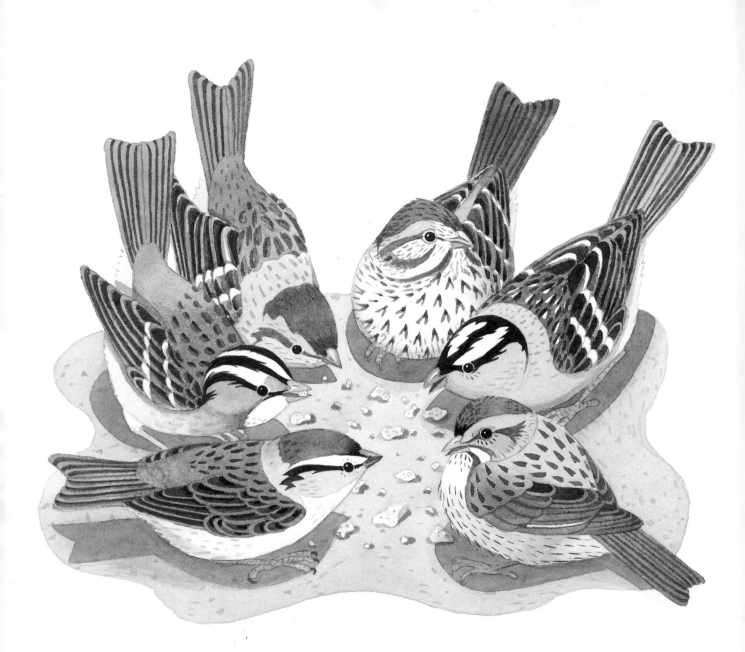

There are lots of little sparrows
hopping around our back door.
They like the bread crumbs I throw
to them each morning.

Today I saw three yellow goldfinches
splashing their feathers clean
in the birdbath in our yard.
A red-eyed vireo came to join them.

Summertime is when swallows
swoop and soar through the sky
searching for mosquitoes to eat.
But the little screech owl
waits in the hole in the oak tree.
When darkness comes, out it flies.

Mourning doves coo and wake me up.

Then the woodpecker starts
to make a loud noise.
It is drilling for insects
in the old maple tree.

The robin begins to sing.
A yellow warbler, a purple finch
and a red-winged blackbird start
to sing their songs.

Mockingbirds and catbirds can imitate
the songs that other birds sing.
The funny catbird can say,
"Meow!" just like a cat.
But the bright Baltimore oriole
has its own pretty song to sing.

Kinglets and nuthatches and chickadees
and juncos and tufted titmice come
to eat the seeds
I put in the bird feeder in winter.

The tiniest bird in our yard
is the ruby-throated hummingbird
that sucks nectar like a bee
from our garden flowers.
The biggest is the big, black raven.

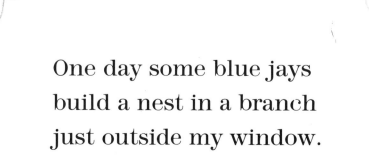

One day some blue jays
build a nest in a branch
just outside my window.

The mother bird lays
four speckled eggs

The eggs hatch into
four baby blue jays!
I watch them every day
from my window.

My father likes the cardinals best.
My mother loves the tiny hummingbirds.
But as for me,

I love every single bird
that I see in our yard.